Unlikely Friends

To Pepper and Ziggy

Our two best beans, today and forever

ISBN: 978-1731-54463-6 paperback

This is a work of fiction. The characters, incidents and dialogue are drawn from the author's imagination and are not to be construed as real. Any resemblance to actual events or persons, living or dead, is entirely coincidental.

Front cover image and book design by Joshua McConnell

Printed by Amazon

First printing edition 2018

babyrhinobooks@gmail.com

Unlikely Friends

Susan Banki

pictures by Joshua McConnell

The yellow sun blazed on the green grassy knoll,
where animals drank at the watering hole.
The parents were teaching their young how to thrive:
where to feed, when to run, what to do to survive.

"The animal kingdom has rules we obey.
We stick with our own and keep others away.
Birds fly with birds, fish swim in the sea.
We stay close together, so just stick with me."

When all of a sudden, quite out of the blue,
the animals gasped, "How can it be true?"
Baby Rhino jumped into the lake with a smack,
with Billy Goat riding on top of her back!

They giggled and snorted and splashed with delight,
told jokes and blew bubbles and had a mud fight.
They hid from each other and then played I Spy.
"Stop mixing with others!" some said with a cry.

"The animal kingdom has rules we obey.
We stick with our own and keep others away.
Birds fly with birds, fish swim in the sea.
A rhino and goat? That just cannot be!"

"What's in it for you?" Zebra questioned the goat,
"Does she help you to swim or perhaps stay afloat?"
"Baby Rhino's my friend. With her I feel free.
It's not just because she does nice things for me."

Giraffe said to Rhino, "Just tell me young tot:
Do you play with that goat 'cause he feeds you a lot?"
"*That goat* is quite smart and he lightens my mood.
I really don't care about presents or food."

Just then, clouds moved in and grew scary and gray.
The rain came down hard and the land washed away.

A great river formed that was deep, cold, and wide,
with animals stuck on the dangerous side.

They huddled in groups and cried out, "This is dire!"
as water rushed higher and higher and higher.

The goat saw a hill and climbed up to the crest,
then looked for dry land where the others could rest.

"It's land!" pointed Goat, standing high on the moss,
so brave Baby Rhino tried swimming across.

"I can't make it alone," she implored with a yelp.
"My friend, I am tired, I really need help."

With all of his strength, Billy Goat pulled her out.
"We must build a boat!" they agreed with a shout.

The goat sketched designs, drawing lines in the sand.
The rhino grabbed leaves from a small patch of land.

The rhino dug mud and the goat chewed at sticks.
They piled on leaves and made waterproof bricks.

And there in the stormy and terrible weather,
the rhino and goat built their vessel together.

The animals scoffed at the newly built craft.
"The rhino can't save us with that flimsy raft!"

Undeterred, she persisted, and struggled to row.
But the boat wouldn't steer; it just rocked to and fro!

Now Rhino was sturdy, courageous and strong.
But tired and frightened, she wouldn't last long.
The goat took a leap and was soon by her side.
"I've fashioned a rudder!" he said with great pride.

While all of the animals watched, full of fear,
the friends grabbed the rudder and started to steer.

"We're saved!" cheered the others, and jumped in the boat.
"Why shouldn't a rhino be friends with a goat?"

From that day to this, dogs and ducks have such fun,
and lions and tigers and bears work as one.

The cheetahs and chimps eat at one yummy feast,
and zebras hang out with the great wildebeest.

The animal kingdom holds many surprises,
chums and companions of all different sizes.

When choosing a friend, look for kindness and laughter.
You'll find that your life's full of joy ever after.

Susan and Josh

Susan and Josh met in Boston, moved to
Australia, and backpacked their way through Asia
and Africa on an extended honeymoon. While
traveling they heard many stories about unlikely
animal friendships, inspiring this story.

It is a sad fact that animals often befriend animals of other species because they are orphaned, which can occur as a result of poaching and loss of natural habitat. As a small part in trying to help slow this unfortunate trend, a portion of all book royalties will be donated to wildlife conservation.

CPSIA information can be obtained
at www.ICGtesting.com
Printed in the USA
LVHW072313010720
659499LV00019B/408